Copyright © 1985 Parker Brothers, Division of CPG Products Corp. All rights reserved. Published in the United States by Parker Brothers, Division of CPG Products Corp.

HUGGA BUNCH is a trademark of Hallmark Cards Inc., used under license.
HUGGA BUNCH designs © 1985 Hallmark Cards Incorporated. All rights reserved.

Library of Congress Cataloging in Publication Data: Creighton, Susan. Huggins and Kisses.
At head of title: Hugga Bunch
SUMMARY: Mary's new puppy, Kisses, seems to be more trouble than he's worth, until a creature from Huggaland shows her how to deal with naughty puppies. 1. Childrens' stories, American.
[1. Dogs — Fiction. 2. Hugging — Fiction]
I. Lipking, Ronald, ill.   II. Title.
PZ7.C8638Hu 1985 [E] 85-5676 ISBN 0-910313-92-X
Manufactured in the United States of America   1 2 3 4 5 6 7 8 9 0   -01

HUGGA BUNCH™

Huggins and Kisses

Story by Susan Creighton
Pictures by Ron C. Lipking

Every morning Mary waved to Mr. Baker from her bedroom window. He would wave back, then walk on with his dog, Sugar, at his heels. Mary would watch the beautiful setter as she waited for her master's signal to cross the street.

"Someday I'll have a dog of my own," Mary said, turning to her old rag doll, Polly. "And he'll be just as well behaved as Sugar. Smart, too. I'll teach him to shake hands and speak and roll over and even fetch a stick."

Mary reached for Polly and gave her a hug.

"Don't worry, Polly," Mary told her. "I'll still love you when I get a dog. After all," she whispered, so the other toys couldn't hear, "you are my favorite!"

Mary kissed Polly on the forehead and together they headed downstairs to the kitchen.

As Mary rounded the corner into the kitchen, she saw her mother and father huddled around something on the floor.

"Mom, Dad, what are you doing?" Mary asked as she came closer. Mary's parents spun around in surprise.

"Trying to tie a big red bow onto this wiggly fur," her father laughed.

Suddenly, a little brown and white bundle scooted out from behind Mary's father and began slipping and sliding every which way. Mary could hardly believe her eyes!

"Daddy! A puppy!" she cried. "Is it really ours?"

"*Yours*, Mary!" her father chuckled. "You've wanted a puppy for so long that Mom and I decided it was high time you had one. Will this little fellow do?"

Mary was already on the floor, hugging the little newcomer. "Oh, Daddy, he's terrific." The puppy was licking Mary's nose, cheeks, and chin. She held Polly out in front of the puppy. "Look, Polly, isn't he cute?" Mary asked. The puppy gave Polly's button nose a lick.

"He certainly is cute," said her mother. "But he's going to be a lot of work, you know."

"We won't mind a bit, will we, Polly?" Mary answered.

She raised the puppy to her nose and looked right into his eyes. "You're just full of kisses, aren't you? Say, how's that for a name? Kisses! Kisses MacDonald!" The puppy wagged his tail and licked Mary's face all over again.

Mary, her mother, and father all burst into laughter.

In the next few days, Mary learned a lot about caring for a puppy. She had to lay newspapers on the floor in case Kisses had an accident. Mary had to brush and feed and walk Kisses several times a day. It *was* work.

Of course, most of the time, Mary and Kisses played together.

Kisses was fun to play with. He loved to chase Mary and was very good at tug-of-war. But sometimes Mary's friends wanted her to play when it was time to feed or walk Kisses. "I can't play just now," she would have to tell them.

Kisses didn't walk on a leash the way Sugar did. He wasn't trained yet. He ran around Mary's legs and got them all tangled up. "Kisses! You've got to behave if you want to walk with me!" Mary scolded. Mary began to wonder if Kisses was ever going to be less work.

Sometimes Kisses was naughty, too. Once he pulled Mary's father's telephone book down and tore all the pages out of it.

"All my important telephone numbers are gone," Mary's father cried. "Mary, you *must* watch Kisses more closely!"

Another time, Kisses dug some holes in the beautiful flower bed Mary's mother had just planted.

"Stop, Kisses!" Mary's mother shouted. But it was too late. "Mary, you have to pay more attention to Kisses," she said.

But the worst thing Kisses did happened one day while Mary was watching television. Kisses found Polly on the living room floor and chewed off her arm before Mary could rescue her.

"Oh, Kisses! How could you!" Mary yelled. Tears filled her eyes. "Get out, you bad dog!"

Kisses scrambled for the door, his tail between his legs, and ran as fast as he could upstairs and hid under Mary's bed.

Mary picked up Polly and hugged her tightly. "My poor Polly," she sobbed, "what has that terrible dog done to you?" Mary ran up to her room, threw herself on the bed, and started crying all over again.

"Don't cry. A hug a day can keep the gloomies away!" said a little voice from Mary's bedpost. "Can I help?"

Mary stopped crying. She sat up and looked around her room. "Who said that?" she asked.

The little visitor jumped off the bedpost, bounced once on the pillow, and landed right in Mary's lap.

"Oh, my!" Mary exclaimed.

"Hello there," said the cute little person. "I'm Huggins, your friend from Huggaland." Mary was surprised. "Where?" she asked.

"It's a magical land right nearby. On the other side of your mirror. And this is Hug-a-Bye," Huggins said, pointing to the tiny creature on her shoulder. "She lives there, too."

These creatures seemed warm and friendly.
"Hello," Mary said, brushing the tears from
her cheeks.

"Looks like you need a hug," Huggins said.

"Thanks," Mary said. "But it'll take more than a
hug to solve my problem. Look!" She held out poor
Polly for Huggins to see.

"You're right. Polly needs help right away, but so do you." Huggins tossed her soft pink curls. "Come on! Follow me," she said.

"Where are we going?" Mary asked.

"To Huggaland," Huggins said. They walked up to the mirror on Mary's closet door and Huggins gave Mary a big hug. The mirror began to change. It started turning all soft and fluffy, like the inside of a cloud.

In a second, Huggins and Hug-a-Bye had stepped
through Mary's mirror. They motioned to Mary to
hurry. Mary clutched Polly tightly, took a deep
breath, and followed.

Kisses had watched Mary talking to Huggins. He was a curious puppy. So just as Mary stepped through the mirror, he darted out from under the bed and followed.

Mary didn't notice Kisses because she was too busy staring at all the wonderful things she saw once she reached the other side of the mirror. "I've never seen so many beautiful, fluffy trees," she said. "And those hills! Why, they look like big, soft quilts!"

"In Huggaland, everything is soft," Huggins said. Then she led the way to her cute little house and sat down in a fluffy pink chair.

"Let me see her," Huggins said, reaching for Polly. She began mending the doll.

Suddenly, there was a loud noise right outside Huggins' window. Mary and Huggins ran to see what had happened.

"It's Kisses!" Mary cried. "He's knocked over your pretty, little pink birdbath!"

Kisses was lapping up the spilled water, and his paws were soaking wet. Mary and Huggins ran out to the scene of the accident.

"What a bad dog you are, Kisses," Mary scolded.
"How could you?"

"Mary, he hasn't really done anything that can't
be fixed," Huggins said gently as she set the birdbath
back in place. "I think he's just thirsty."

Huggins filled a bowl with water and set it down in front of Kisses. Then she gave him a big, soft hug. "There now, isn't that better?" she said.

Mary pulled Polly closer. "How can you hug Kisses when he's been such a bad puppy?" she asked.

"All puppies are naughty sometimes," Huggins replied. "But even when they are, they still need loving hugs. And with a little gentle discipline, a puppy can grow up to be a good pet and a wonderful friend."

Mary scratched her head. "I really want Kisses to be my friend, but…"

"And he will be, Mary. Kisses just hasn't had time to learn everything you want him to know," said Huggins.

"I guess I haven't been very patient with him.
I'm sure glad you came by to help me!" She threw
her arms around Huggins and gave her a great big
thank-you hug.

Huggins giggled. "Two hugs are better than one, I always say!" She hugged Mary back, and then gave Polly a tender little hug. "And look, Polly's as good as new!"

Mary bent down next to Kisses. "Kisses, we're going to be even better friends starting right now," said Mary, hugging him with all her might. "Come on, let's go home. I'll fix you an extra special treat for lunch!" Kisses licked Mary's face all over.

Mary and Kisses started heading toward the fluffy mirror that would bring them back home. Mary stopped and turned back to Huggins. "I can't thank you enough," she said. "I had almost forgotten how much I love Kisses."

"Aw, it's all in a day's hugs, Mary!" Huggins
blushed. "All in a day's hugs!"